Admiration

By

Jerusha Moors

CHAPTER ONE

Lady Selina Masters trained her eyes out the window at the passing scenery. The day looked raw and blustery, no snow yet, but it wouldn't be long before it covered the ground. She hoped to see some before Christmas; Selina relished walking through crisp snow when they went to cut pine boughs and collect holly for decorating. It was one of her favorite activities for the holiday season.

A whistling snort from her mother seated next to her in the traveling carriage had her turn to check on her. Her mother, the Dowager Countess of Ludlow, was sleeping, her chin resting on her prodigious bosom and her breath ruffling the fur on her traveling cape.

Selina loved her mother, but she wished that she hadn't insisted on attending the house party at Wakefield Hall but gone to spend the holidays at Ludlow Abbey as they usually did. William, her brother and now the Earl of Ludlow, was there with his family and would have gladly hosted his mother, but she insisted on accompanying Selina as a chaperone. She had complained the entire trip even though William's coach was most comfortable and well-sprung.

Her mother hoped to find a husband for Selina at the house party. Selina's pleas that Anne, the Countess of Wakefield, had indicated it would be a small party of intimate friends and family did not dissuade her. She didn't even try to argue her firm belief there was no possibility of her finding a husband regardless. Selina might be the daughter and sister to an Earl, but she was firmly on the shelf, at least in her mind. She had spent all the time in London looking for a husband she intended despite her mother's wringing of hands.

Another snort and her mother shifted and lifted her head, her eyes bleary with fatigue.

"I did not understand Wakefield Hall was so far else I'd have stayed at Ludlow," she complained as she straightened her bonnet. "I'm too old for all this traveling about at this time of year."

Selina suppressed a sigh. That was precisely the argument she had tried to make, and that her mother had disregarded it. All she'd wanted was to spend quiet time with Anne and her family. Instead, she would need to entertain her mother, cosset her, and be at her beck and call — not that Selina begrudged caring for her mother. It was just that she'd hoped for a little time to herself.

"I believe we're almost there," she responded. "When we stopped at that last inn, John Coachman said we should arrive around mid-afternoon."

"Bevins, wake up," her mother ordered sharply. The maid slumped in the corner opposite Selina, curled into a ball on the forward seat.

"Yes, my lady, I'm awake." The maid sat up straight and blinking her eyes, fussing with her skirts. She leaned forward to adjust the Countess's bonnet, so it tilted over her forehead.

The Countess nodded, then looked her daughter over. "I wish you wouldn't wear such drab colors, Selina. Those dark colors don't suit your youth."

Selina bit the inside of her cheek. "I'm twenty-four years old, Mama, no longer a debutante in my first season. These colors are appropriate for my age and station."

Bevins looked down at the carriage floor, studying her toes and hoping her opinion wouldn't be asked. Selina knew her mother's longtime maid had sympathy for her, but she would never interfere between mother and daughter.

Before her mother could react to her statement, the coach slowed and turned. Selina glanced out the window. "We have arrived at Wakefield Hall."

They pulled up to a two-story Georgian mansion made of light stone. It was plain, and the Countess sniffed as she caught sight of the house, but Selina loved it at first sight. It was the perfect home for Anne and her husband, Richard, not too ostentatious while still having accommodations for many guests. Set in the park on a small rise, it exuded warmth and charm.

Another coach had arrived before them, and there was a crowd of people at the front door. Selina spotted Anne on the steps, her husband at her side talking to two other men and a woman. They looked up at the arriving carriage and waited for them despite the cold weather. Selina recognized the Duke of Carlisle, the tall, ginger-haired man talking to Richard so she thought the woman must be his new wife, but she didn't know their companion.

Richard came to greet them and open their door, disdaining the help of a servant. He helped the Countess down, but it was the other man who had been standing with them who came forward to aid Selina.

"My lady," he said as he took her hand. Selina felt the warm touch of his hand right through her gloves, and she looked up, not taking her usual care as she disembarked from the coach. She glimpsed dark eyes in a rugged face as her bad leg gave out and she pitched forward. Selina closed her eyes, expecting an impact with the gravel, but the man caught her and hauled her back, dignity impaired but safe from injury.

"My lady!" Bevins called. "You forgot your cane."

Selina closed her eyes, drawing in a deep breathe. How very humiliating. She had been in such a hurry to remove herself from the confines of the carriage and greet her friend she forgot her affliction.

Her cheeks turned red as she realized the stranger was still supporting her with his arm around her waist.

"Are you all right?" he asked in a bass rumble. He smelled of bay rum and something indefinably male as he continued to hold her upright. He must have heard Bevins, and Selina felt humiliated at the thought this stranger knew her stumble was not just a turn of her foot.

"I'm fine, thank you." Selina turned, trying to break away from his hold, but his arm clamped around her waist. "Thank you, Bevins. I quite forgot." She held out a hand for the cane, her neck growing hot as she tried to ignore the man holding onto her. "How very foolish of me."

She put the tip of the cane into the gravel and stepped away though those hawk eyes never left her figure, apparently worried that she would take another tumble onto the driveway. He was ready to catch her if she fell again, evidently not trusting her cane. By this time her mother and Anne had rushed to her aid, and the stranger stepped back next to the Duke of Carlisle.

"Oh, Selina, I'm so sorry." Anne was apologetic while her mother fussed over her, rearranging her pelisse and bonnet as if she were a small child again, much to Selina's dismay. She was sure her face was redder than holly berries.

"Really, it's all right. I should have paid more attention to what I was doing. It is quite my fault." Selina fixed a smile on her face, determined not to show her mortification. This was *not* the way she wished to begin her visit.

Richard held out an arm and Selina gratefully took hold. Her bad leg seemed to have survived the wrench, but she knew it might give out again at any moment. She limped next to the Earl as he led her up the stairs to the front door. She could feel all eyes on her, but she would not look to see who gazed with pity. Her mother still fluttered about as the rest of the party followed them into the house.

"I believe Anne has tea ready in the drawing room if you'd like something after your journey," Richard murmured to her. "Or perhaps you'd rather retire to your chambers for a rest."

"Tea would be perfect, my lord," Selina answered, her chin held high. Richard and Anne knew of her infirmity and never treated her differently than another, but she didn't know the rest of the party. The man who had caught her hadn't judged her, she thought, but then he probably thought she had just tripped or had an injury from a recent fall. He didn't know how damaged she was — yet.

Richard relieved her of her pelisse, gloves, and bonnet, handing them off to a servant, then settled her on a sofa. Anne came to sit next to her, squeezing her hand in greeting as the rest of the party took seats around the room. It was a comfortable setting, a fire burning in the grate, with chairs and the sofa set to take advantage of the heat. The Duke ensured that her mother was in the chair closest to the fireplace.

A maid brought the tea set in just as Lucy, Richard's sister, and her husband, Aubrey, Viscount Lovell, appeared. Selina noted that while Lucy was as beautiful as ever, she seemed with child. The Duchess of Carlisle also seemed to be in a family way. It made sense as both women had recently married, but a familiar pang hurt her heart, just for a moment. Pushing her thoughts away, she straightened her posture as befitted a lady before her mother noticed.

Anne busied herself with pouring tea while Richard introduced those in the party who didn't know each other and handed out the cups for his wife.

"I believe you might recognize this tall man with the Scottish accent, our dear friend, the Duke of Carlisle, and his wife." Selina had seen the Duke in London but did not know him well. His wife was a pleasant-looking woman with dark chestnut hair. She had heard the woman had married above her, but Selina didn't think Anne would be friendly with a social climber. The Duchess nodded to her with a warm smile.

"Of course, you know my sister, but you may not have met her husband, Viscount Lovell, who is also our neighbor." The Viscount was a handsome man who stood behind his wife's chair watching over her with careful solicitude.

Anne broke in. "And our latest arrivals are her ladyship, the Countess of Ludlow, and her daughter — and my dearest friend — Lady Selina Masters. We are delighted to have you join us for this festive season."

Richard brought a cup of tea to the man who had not yet been introduced and clapped him on the shoulder. The man was standing off to himself in a corner, quietly observing the company.

"And lest we forget, here is my new acquaintance and the Duke's good friend, Mr. Gray of Edinburgh."

Selina gave the man a smile, but her mother ignored him, just giving him a cursory glance.

"Is this the entire party then?" the Dowager Countess of Ludlow asked. She pursed her lips, and Selina's heart sank. Her mother would be difficult and embarrassing.

"Mama, perhaps you'd like to rest before dinner?" she said, hoping to deflect her complaints about the lack of eligible men at the party.

"Of course, my lady," Anne joined in. "You have had a long journey, and we have readied a comfortable chamber for you."

Selina took her cane and pushed off the sofa, steadying herself on Anne's shoulder. "Yes, Mama. I could use a rest also, and I'd like to refresh myself after our travels."

Richard crossed the room and helped her mother. They hadn't left her with much choice, Selina thought with a sigh of relief. Not that her mother was an objectionable person. It was instead that she was like a dog with a bone. Her only aim in life now was to settle her daughter with a titled husband despite Selina's resistance.

Selina nodded at the others but obediently followed Richard and her mother out of the room. In truth, she wasn't tired, and she would have liked to have spent more time with Anne and the rest of the party, but it would be better to get her mother settled now. Perhaps Mama's mood would improve after a nap, and then Selina could look forward to a less fractious evening.

She was conscious Mr. Gray had a frown on his face as he watched her limp out of the room. Selina straightened her back and held her head up. It was always difficult with new people who weren't used to her abnormality. They didn't know how to treat her, whether to cosset her or pretend to ignore her lame leg.

She passed out of the room, but Selina stopped when she heard the deep bass of Mr. Gray. "Does the lady need any aid in climbing the stairs?"

She closed her eyes, unaccountably sad at his question which was silly since she didn't even know the man. She heard the soft murmur of Anne's voice, and she proceeded down the hall as fast as she could go, her cane tapping as she went.

CHAPTER TWO

"Lady Selina is quite independent, Mr. Gray. She does not welcome help unless she requests it." Anne held up a hand as he attempted to remonstrance and he subsided. "She will ask if she feels she needs help. The incident as she stepped down from her coach was an aberration, I assure you."

Eleanor, Duchess of Carlisle, put her teacup on a side table. "Is it a recent injury?"

Anne looked at the doorway, shaking her head slowly. "No, Lady Selina was afflicted as a child. There was a teething fever that caused her left leg to lose strength. The weakness in the limb has been longstanding."

Lucy took a scone with a mischievous look at her husband but sobered as she responded, "I have always liked Lady Selina. You and she grew up together, did you not, Anne?"

"Yes, we were neighbors in Shropshire. We have always enjoyed a good friendship, so I am delighted she agreed to visit. Selina would rather stay at home at Ludlow Abbey. She has always been...shy."

Aubrey, Viscount Lovell, frowned. "I imagine her Season was difficult."

Lucy agreed with her husband. "Dancing is a required activity in the Ton. People can be most unkind to anyone who doesn't fit in."

Aubrey placed a hand on his wife's shoulder and squeezed. Lucy had endured an unpleasant Season of her own in her time though that was all behind them now.

Mr. Gray shifted, placing his teacup on the table next to him. "I apologize, Lady Anne. I meant no disrespect, but only meant to aid the lady if she needed it."

Anne smiled sweetly at her guest. "Of course, sir. It is very thoughtful of you to ask. I also thank you for your earlier service in assisting Lady Selina out of the carriage. You possibly prevented a serious mishap."

He nodded, his cheeks flushed as he picked up his teacup once more. Jamie, the Duke of Carlisle, walked over to his friend.

"David, I add my thanks for your assistance with Lady Selina. It would have been a shame if her stumble had seriously injured her."

"I happened to be in the right place at the right time." He fidgeted with the teacup as Jamie studied him, but then the Duke changed the subject.

"Eleanor and I are happy you could come with us here for the holiday season and meet our friends," he whispered.

David cleared his throat nervously. "I did not expect that all would be...titled. It's disconcerting for a man of my rank."

Jamie looked around the room, startled by the remark. Though a Duke, his wife was not of noble stock and he did not make much of a person's rank.

"Truth be told, while most here come from titled families, not one person here thinks much of it beyond the responsibilities they hold to their people. You may be a new acquaintance to them, but I think you will find them to be generous and kind, not at all snobbish."

A corner of his mouth tipped up as David smiled. "I thank you again for inviting me. Everyone has been most warm in their greetings and very welcoming."

"When I heard you intended to stay alone at your home for the holidays and mentioned it to Eleanor, she at once asked if you could join us. She thinks a lot of you and is most distressed to think you might be all alone while we enjoyed our Yuletide celebrations."

David put his teacup down once more, hiding his face from his friend. That the Duke and Duchess treated him as an equal touched him. They had met when David helped the Duke with some business investments, and the two men had hit it off. The Duke's primary residence was in Carlisle where David's offices and home also were sited though he also had a house in Edinburgh, so they saw a lot of each other, especially as the Duchess preferred her home there to the smog and noise of London.

At that moment Eleanor rose and approached the men, a sweet smile on her face for her husband. David felt a pang seeing the love between the couple. It was rare for members of the Ton to find love in marriage as most unions were arranged for prestige and money, but the group in this room were different. Each of the three couples here had married for love.

"David, may I borrow my husband for a moment? I'd like to settle in after our journey today, and I could use his aid." Eleanor's creamy skin flushed prettily, and Jamie arched an eyebrow as he absorbed her words.

"Of course, your Grace," David replied, amused at the question. They were newlyweds, after all.

"Please, here we are all using first names, no titles for the nonce. Please call me Eleanor."

David nodded, pleased with her kind gesture. The other ladies had also risen to visit the nursery while their husbands prepared to repair to the pool room for a game or two. Richard called to David, "Would you like to join us? We would like to talk more with you. Jamie has been telling us some interesting tales of your ventures together."

"I thank you and would be most glad to speak with you at a later time this week, if possible," David replied. "I think I would prefer to stretch my legs now after the carriage ride. Some fresh air before dinner will suit me if that does not disrupt your plans."

"Indeed, feel free to wander the grounds as you wish. Perhaps you can scout out greenery for decorations. The ladies will have us outdoors in the next few days to bring in holly and boughs to decorate the hall."

Richard and Aubrey followed their wives out of the room while Jamie tarried for a moment, just to be sure he wasn't abandoning his friend, but at a nod from David, he followed his wife out.

With a glance out the window at the gray skies, David went to get his coat. No matter the weather, a stroll would be refreshing.

AFTER ENSURING THAT her mother was comfortable in her spacious room, Selina quickly unpacked her own things. She knew if she waited, Bevins would be by to hang up her clothes, but meanwhile, her mother would monopolize all of the maid's time. They were supposed to share Bevins, an economy that her brother bemoaned as there was no need for it. Selina didn't mind doing for herself though, and she enjoyed her privacy. She didn't want someone fussing over her most of the time, and it suited her that Bevins would help her when she needed it, but left her alone otherwise.

Selina walked over to the window and gazed out at the park beyond. Though the day was still overcast, she thought it would be more restful to go out for a walk even if the garden beds were covered and dead rather than to take a nap before dinner. Her leg ached from the enforced sit in the carriage, and if Selina didn't walk very far, it would feel good to stretch it. She took her cane, pelisse, hat, and gloves and made her way down the hall and stairs. A few servants eyed her as she passed, but no one spoke or stopped her.

She left through the front door and followed a path around the house to the back where she carefully walked down the rows, leaning on her cane as she trod the uneven ground. Selina headed towards a small copse of trees where she could see a small gazebo. In the summer it would be lovely to sit and read under the shade of the trees, but now the building was a solitary respite from the wind.

Reaching it, she sank down on the bench and rubbed at her sore knee. The wrench from her trip when she got down from the carriage had aggravated it, but Selina was thankful that it was not a more severe injury. Now she was here, she did not want to miss any time with her friends.

Mr. Gray had been most attentive, she mused. And helpful. Selina sighed. She didn't like he had seen her disability so plainly, but she couldn't help it. That was the penalty for venturing out in public. Perhaps he could accept it like a gentleman and not mention it or become over-solicitous.

She hated pity.

Unfortunately, she was also used to it. Or scorn. Many of the girls who had their debut with her had preferred to treat her with contempt rather than thinly-veiled charity. Selina preferred the scorn, not that it mattered. Her leg was the way it was, and all the doctors who had treated her over the years were consistent in the belief it couldn't be mended.

She shivered, a gust of wind reminding her she had been sitting for a while. She picked up her cane and rose, ready to return to the house. At the least, her knee felt better for the slight exercise.

She was partway through the garden when a dog appeared. It was large with matted, dirty hair. It looked like a stray, rather skinny, and not a friendly one that might hope for a handout.

Selina halted, steadying herself with her walking stick. If the dog attacked, she could try to hold it away with her cane, but she doubted that would work for long. She couldn't outrun the animal for a certainty.

Looking up, she saw a movement off to her right. Mr. Gray was coming toward them, his hands up in a motion for her to stay still. Selina swallowed hard, nodded, and looked back down at the beast in front of her.

The dog didn't show its teeth but moved closer to her, limping on one front paw. Selina held her ground, determined to show no fear. Mr.

Gray was still not close though she wasn't sure what he could do anyway if the dog attacked.

The animal whined softly and held up a paw. Selina scrunched up her nose, puzzled by the action. She wasn't used to dogs though she loved animals. Her mother felt that a dog might trip her and injure her weak leg more, so she forbade a pet, but Selina cozened any animal she came across.

Slowly, using her cane to help her balance, she sank to the ground. Her knee protested, but Selina ignored the pang. The dog moved closer, whining as it put his paw down on the ground. She carefully reached out and gently picked up the sore paw.

Mr. Gray had arrived about ten paces away, panting from running across the lawn. Selina looked up and shook her head slightly, indicating that he should stand back. He looked worried, but he obeyed her.

"There, boy, what have you done to yourself?" she crooned to the beast. Its large brown eyes looked hopefully at her. Mr. Gray made a small noise, but he stayed where he was, and the dog ignored him, his eye fixed on Selina.

"Will you let me see your paw?" She was holding it, but now she looked down to examine it for wounds. Dried blood marked the fur between two claws, so she pulled the toes apart. Selina couldn't see anything, but she felt a thin needle-like stick or thorn caught in the skin there. She carefully grasped it and pulled it out. The dog never moved but licked at its paw, then her hand.

"Outstanding work, Lady Selina."

Mr. Gray had approached while she was working on the injury, and he squatted on the lawn next to her. Selina had forgotten about him, but she wasn't pleased that he had observed her interactions with the dog. *A lady wouldn't sit on the cold ground to help a hurt animal, or for any reason,* she thought she could hear her mother's voice. But the man appeared when she least wanted him near though she could grudgingly admit that he was helpful.

"Well, he seems a good dog, just needs food and care. If I can get him up to the house, I'd like to clean both him and the wound if it's possible."

The dog put his head in her lap, spreading mud across her pelisse, but she didn't mind.

MR. GRAY CHUCKLED. "I believe this particular lion will do anything you ask, Lady Selina." David rose and helped Selina to her feet, taking her hand to pull her up.

"Lion, Mr. Gray?" She ruffled the fur behind the animal's ears, and the dog leaned into her caress. David watched her hand and had the startling wish she'd run her hand through his hair. He coughed to cover his confusion at the thought. He had only just met the woman.

"Yes, have you heard the old story of Androcles and the Lion? He pulls a thorn from the lion's paw and makes a friend for life." He took her arm to help her to her feet, and they started up toward the house, the dog obediently walking beside Selina.

"Of course, yes, I've heard the tale." Selina laughed, and David let the sound warm him. "That could be a good name for this dog, at least until someone claims him."

"Lion? I agree," David responded, charmed by her humor. "But I suspect that Lion may be a stray. He's certainly bedraggled enough."

"Oh, dear. I don't suppose Anne will be happy about this." A small smile tipped up the corner of Selina's mouth, a motion that David found mesmerizing.

He shook his head. "The Countess seems a very obliging woman. I'm sure you don't have to worry about her sensibilities in the matter." He cleared his throat. "Indeed, if no one claims him, and you don't have a place for him, perhaps I could solve this problem for you."

"You would take him home with you, Mr. Gray?" Selina's eyes were wide, but she had a hopeful look.

Actually, David had meant that he would find a farm that would take the dog in. A large dog such as this would not manage well in his home in Carlisle nor in the townhouse in Edinburgh. Therefore, he surprised himself when he said, "I would be pleased to take in such a fine companion as Lion."

Selina didn't seem to notice any confusion on his part. She patted the dog's head, a pleased smile on her face.

"That is very kind of you, Mr. Gray. I'm sure it would thrill your children to have such a noble friend as Lion."

He paused, and Selina turned. They hadn't been walking fast anyway, but she held onto his arm to steady herself, and it mortified David that he hadn't thought of her leg.

"Your pardon, Lady Selina. I didn't mean to stop so abruptly." He glanced away, up toward the house and walked again. In a quieter tone, he said, "I have no wife or children. I expect Lion will fill that void for me, at least for the present."

Selina blushed. "Forgive me, Mr. Gray. I did not mean to imply...to suggest...I'm sorry," she stopped and bit her lip.

"You have nothing to apologize for, Lady Selina. I am a businessman, and I spend most of my days working, with no time for a family." He frowned, the thought displeasing him. "I am an ordinary man, but the Duke has taken notice of me. He was very kind to have included me in the invitation this week." He shrugged. "I believe he thought I was spending too many hours at work."

"Then he will be glad you have the distraction of a dog to ease some of your burdens. I don't know him well, but Anne thinks very highly of him."

David ducked his head, embarrassed at the praise. "Perhaps Lion's owner will turn up."

Selina raised an eyebrow in mock reproof, and David hastily added, "Of course, I would be despondent if that happened."

He grinned when she let out a peal of laughter, enjoying her sense of humor and honesty. David enjoyed everything about her, in fact, and that had him worried. He couldn't recall the last time he had taken so quickly to a person. He tended to be stand-offish, a bit prickly and didn't readily trust someone until he knew them for a while. It was his upbringing, an only child in a strict household of just his father and himself. His teacher father never remarried after his wife's death when David was seven, but devoted himself to educating his son and pushing him to make something better of himself than a rural teacher.

"Perhaps we should enter by a back door," Selina suggested. "Anne is tolerant, but I don't want to create more work for her servants by bringing Lion in through the front entrance."

"I agree. Or perhaps I should take Lion down to the stables and deal with his mud there."

"A much better idea, sir. But surely you would have the stable boys do the bathing?" Selina frowned, her lips pursed as she regarded his wool coat and leather gloves.

"I will assist, my lady, and perhaps you'd supervise, just to determine that Lion has no more wounds that need treating." It was bold of David to ask Selina to come to the stables; she was a lady after all, not a farmer's wife. He started to revoke his suggestion, but she didn't look horrified at the idea and spoke before he took back his words.

"I would be happy to supervise Lion's bath." She was beaming, a broad smile on her face.

It puzzled David until he recalled Anne's words about Selina's independence. By asking her to help him with the dog, he had inadvertently appealed to her sense of self-sufficiency. That was more important to her than the appearance of propriety. The lady probably did not have much opportunity to act outside the strictures of her society or without hovering over her because of her bad leg, at least judging by her mother's actions.

They turned and headed off to the back of the house where the stables were housed. David kept an eye on Selina's pace, not hurrying, but not coddling her either. She seemed recovered from her almost tumble at her arrival.

Her mind must also have been on her injury. They had walked a short distance in silence when she spoke, her eyes fixed on the barns ahead.

"I was ill as a child, a fever that affected my limbs. It has caused one leg to be weak." She blushed; a lady would never speak of her legs in mixed company, but David thought her brave and all the more a lady. He knew it must cost her dearly to explain to him; she was not a person who looked for pity.

David thought carefully as to his response. Her cheeks flamed brighter, but she strode along determinedly, faster than she should.

"I admire you, my lady."

Selina stopped but did not turn her face to him. Her shoulders tensed as the grip of her arm on his tightened. Lion whined softly, sensing his new owner's stress.

"Why, if I may ask? You don't even know me."

David swallowed, nervous that he had offended though her tone was quiet, not haughty. "Because you would care for a stray dog. Because you are gracious to a gentleman far below you in rank and without the manners of your usual associates. And because you do not look for pity though many others might in your circumstances."

Startled, Selina looked up. David met her eyes as she studied him.

"Thank you," she whispered. The tension eased from her body, and her arm relaxed on his as Lion started ahead, turning his head to see if they would follow.

CHAPTER THREE

Selina sat on a hard wooden chair that one of the stable-hands had found somewhere in the depths of the building and watched as Lion stood in his bath. True to his word, Mr. Gray had supervised the boys as they set up the large tub, but Lion wouldn't enter the water until his new owner took off his coat and waistcoat, rolled up the fine linen sleeves of his shirt, and knelt next to the tub.

Lion submitted patiently to the scrubbing though the two boys initially assigned to do the washing stood nearby, ready to foil any possible escape attempts by the dog. David examined the animal carefully, but the only real hurt the dog suffered was the sore paw that Selina had already taken care of.

"Hand me that blanket to dry him off please, Tobias," David ordered one boy who dutifully gave him an old brown covering used for the horses. He stood up, and Lion took that as a sign it released him. He jumped out of the tub and shook himself before David could step back, dousing him with water.

The wet linen clung to his form displaying a manly chest of dark hair. He had broad shoulders and his form tapered to a trim waist. Selina could not look away though she knew as a lady she should.

Laughing, David picked at the shirt until he saw that Lion was ready for another shake, so he hastily threw the blanket over the animal. As he pulled the wet shirt away from his torso, he looked up and caught Selina's rapt gaze. His eyes grew hot as if he knew what she was thinking and uncomfortable, she looked away. Her cheeks grew warm, and she fumbled for her cane, ready to escape both the barn and her embarrassing thoughts.

The boys were rubbing Lion with the blanket, but David was still watching her as if he'd forgotten his damp clothing or the shrieks arising from the trio behind him. Selina swallowed, then firmed her jaw as she stood. Thank goodness the rigidity of the chair gave her something to push off from and remain steady on her feet while the cane kept her from overbalancing.

What would her mother think? She had only known this man for a few hours, and now she was eying him in a manner that would appall Miss Lewis, her old governess, who had molded her to be the lady her mother expected her to be. Sitting in a stable and ogling a gentleman's chest wasn't at all proper.

"I need to return to the house. The gong for dinner will ring soon, and I must dress." She kept her eyes turned away from David and started for the doors as fast as she could move. Selina knew she sounded abrupt, almost rude, but he would understand how improper this situation was. Too bad she hadn't realized it sooner, and color flamed her cheeks once more.

"Lady Selina, please wait," came the call behind her. "Let me escort you back to the house."

"I'm perfectly fine, thank you," she called over her shoulder, hating that he would observe her limping gait. "Please finish with Lion, and I'll see you at dinner."

She hurried on, glad she had made her escape and wanting time to examine her feelings. Mr. Gray had discombobulated her, though to be fair it was not his fault. He was only doing as she asked in taking on the dog, and to be fair, a dog that was not his responsibility.

No, Selina thought. *I'm just tired after the journey and not thinking properly.*

She didn't see David watching her leave as he slowly rolled his sleeves back down, his head tilted thoughtfully until Lion whined and pushed him.

"I know, boy, you miss her already." He patted the dog's head absently, consumed by thoughts of the surprising Lady Selina. Then he reached for his jacket. "Let us see if we can find a place for you in the kitchen until I speak to Lady Anne. And I must hurry to change also, or I will be late for dinner."

BEVINS HELPED SELINA into her dark green dinner dress edged with gold lace, one of her favorites. She arranged her brown hair up in a loose mass of curls with the gold pins topped with cunning small roses scattered among the tendrils of hair. She knew she looked well, but pushed aside any thoughts of why she cared. It was just a dinner with friends, people she knew well mostly.

She blushed as she thought once more of Mr. Gray in his wet shirt. She hadn't been able to remove that vision from her mind, one that no real lady should have ever seen. Why had she gone with him into the barn anyway?

The maid pushed the last pin into the back of her hair and stood back. "You look very nice, Lady Selina if I say so myself. That color suits you no matter what your mother might say."

Bevins had been with her mother for many years and felt entitled to speak her mind. Selina was used to her bluntness and trusted her opinions.

"Do you think so?" she asked. "I've always liked it." She pulled one curl down over her ear, then rolled her eyes as Bevins shook her head and tucked it back into her coiffure.

"You look lovely," Bevins said. "Do you want the gold eardrops? You usually wear them with this dress."

"Yes, please. That'll do." Selina took them from the maid and inserted them into her ears. "Now I'll just check on my mother before I go down for dinner."

"Her ladyship is fine, Lady Selina. She'll take a tray in her room, and then read until she falls asleep. She's just tired out from the long journey."

Selina nodded absently and took the shawl Bevins handed her. She peeked into the room across the hall where her mother lodged but closed the door again when she saw only a large lump in the bed. The journey had worn her mother out, and Selina felt guilty. Perhaps she should have stayed with William and his family for the holiday, but it was her mother's choice to accompany her. Selina could have made the journey herself comfortably, and her brother would have ensured she had a companion or maid to keep her company.

Well, it was too late now. Her mother was here, and she would endure Mama's querulousness. Hopefully, it wouldn't disconcert her friends. Yes, Anne knew her mother well.

Sighing, she descended the stairs and entered the drawing room where the others were waiting. She hated to be the last one to arrive somewhere. It left her disability on display when all eyes looked at her entrance. She bit her lip and stopped right inside the door, knowing she could limp in once everyone returned to their conversations.

It surprised her when Mr. Gray came forward and took her arm, drawing her to a sofa where Anne sat talking to Eleanor. Selina felt a flash of irritation he thought she needed the aid but then felt shamed. He was merely acting the gentleman.

He helped her to sit, then withdrew to a position near the fireplace where the Duke was standing speaking with Aubrey. Richard and Lucy, across the room, were involved in the type of discussion that only close siblings had. Selina could recognize it from her own relationship with her brother William.

Anne turned with a smile. "How is your mother, Selina? I asked that a tray be sent up to her, one I hope tempts her appetite."

"Mama is still resting, but I'm sure she'll be delighted with whatever you give her. No one in my family is a fussy eater, as you well know."

Anne laughed and patted Selina's arm. "We country folk have hearty appetites. Richard is dangerous when a roast is served, and I've hidden my sweets away to hoard them for myself."

Eleanor nodded. "I'm partial to sponge cake and jam myself. It's one of my favorite parts of the Christmas holidays."

"I'm sure that Cook is planning to serve plenty of sponge cake. It is popular in our dining room also."

William, the tiny Welsh butler at Wakefield Hall, entered the room to announce dinner was ready. Each couple found each other which left Selina with Mr. Gray once more. He smiled and held out an arm, and they followed the others into the dining room. The seating was informal, and they took the last two seats next to each other with Selina on Anne's right.

It seemed they were paired off.

Selina felt herself blushing at the thought. She didn't think she had blushed so much in years. Undoubtedly it was just a convenience with them being the last twosome even though they were nearly strangers. A vision of Mr. Gray in his wet shirt popped into her head and she felt her blush grow hotter. Oh, dear, maybe not such strangers then.

"You look recovered, Lady Selina," Mr. Gray interrupted her thought.

"Recovered?" What did the man mean? Could he have read her thoughts in the barn?

"From your travels," he answered. "I hope your mother is feeling better."

"Oh, yes, she is taking a tray in her room, but I believe she will be up and about tomorrow."

Mr. Gray nodded and wrinkled his forehead. He gave her a weak smile and nodded once more. Selina could not make him out. Next, he would talk about the weather. She had found him able to speak of more interesting matters earlier.

"I left Lion in the good care of the stable boys."

Good, not the weather. "I should tell Anne about him." She turned to speak to Anne, but Mr. Gray interrupted her.

"No need, I already spoke to Lady Anne."

"David, I thought we agreed we are all friends and should address ourselves by our first names." Anne must have heard them conversing despite her own conversation with Aubrey who sat across from Selina.

"Of course...Anne. I meant no disrespect. I was merely confirming to Lady Selina that I had already spoken to you about the dog."

Anne glanced at Selina, one eyebrow lifted, and Selina felt the mental prod. They always could read each other's mind.

"Please, I am Selina. And you are..."

"David." He swallowed hard, and Selina watched his throat move above his snowy white ascot. He dressed impeccably, as fine as any of the other gentlemen, and why not? He was a gentleman, even if not titled.

Selina turned back to find both Anne and Aubrey looking at the pair of them. Anne had a curious look, but Aubrey was definitely smirking as if he knew something no one else knew.

A frisson of discomfort ran down her spine. Mr. Gray, or rather, David, was very nice. He had helped her with Lion and escorted her about today, but that meant nothing. She was the only unmatched female here, and he was polite, a kind man. No one should read anything into him doing his duty.

She looked down into her lap, pretending to adjust her napkin. When she looked up again, Aubrey had launched into a story about his daughter, Annabelle, and her pony. Selina knew from Anne's letters he had only discovered the existence of his daughter the year before, and tiny Annabelle had wound her besotted papa firmly around her finger.

Selina gradually relaxed though she was acutely aware of the man seated next to her. When she turned her head, she caught the faint scent of bay rum she'd noticed on David earlier in the day. Perhaps it was her imagination, but she seemed to feel the heat from his body along her right side, much more than she had ever noticed from any other man sitting next to her as a dinner companion. Too often gentlemen of the Ton had a more unpleasant odor.

She moved the food around her plate, too nervous to eat. Selina was bewildered at her confusion. She was with dear friends, but right now she wished to be alone in her own room at Ludlow Abbey. Her feelings were very perplexing.

"Are you not hungry, my lady?" David asked her in a low tone.

She gave him a wry smile. "The food is delicious, but I'm afraid I'm overtired after my journey."

"Selina, you don't have to eat if you don't wish." Anne had overheard their conversation again.

"Perhaps I should retire. I would like to be fresh for tomorrow's festivities. Right now I feel like a wilted flower."

"Nay, Selina, perhaps like a calendula or tulip that rests at night to rise again in beauty as the sun shines."

Selina froze, sure her face was as bright as David's once he realized what he said. It was clear from his embarrassment he gotten carried away. Her impression of him was a quiet, businesslike man. Perhaps the journey fatigued him also, or unused to company.

Anne came to the rescue. "How poetically you speak, David, and quite profoundly also. It is very true our Selina shines, night or day."

David stood and bowed his head. "Yes, my lady, erm, Anne."

The poor man looked confounded, and Selina felt a twinge of pity amid her own mortification. David pushed his chair back, his back straight and held his arm out to her.

"Oh, I can..." Selina's voice trailed off as she looked around the table, realizing that everyone was watching their little tableau. "Thank you, David."

She stood and took his arm, biting her lip. His arm was rigid under hers, and she knew he was just as happy to leave the room as she. They went with good wishes ringing in their ears.

Once they were in the hallway, Selina felt David relax. He halted at the bottom of the stairs and turned to her. He closed his eyes and took a deep breath. Once he composed himself, he spoke.

"Selina, I must apologize for my intemperate words. I can only plead fatigue from my journey."

A twinge of disappointment unsettled her stomach. "I thought perhaps that was the reason for your..." she searched for the correct word, "*poetic* musings. We should have both settled for trays in our rooms this evening."

A frown wrinkled his brow. "I meant what I said. You look beautiful this evening." He turned red again and sighed. "I've done it again. I mean only to compliment you. I'm not usually so clumsy with my words."

She patted his arm. "It's all right, sir. After all, I owe you for your care of Lion."

"Yes, but I'm delighted to take charge of the dog. His manner grows on one, I confess, though I fear I won't be able to keep up with his feedings. I must work extra hours or take on additional work." He laughed, a deep chuckle, and Selina smiled in response. She had never had an issue with a man who worked for his living. Her brother and most of the other men she knew invested and ran their estates. Some of the Ton looked down on those 'in trade,' but the dirty secret was that many of them depended on them to manage their investments.

"Perhaps I will need to send you mutton bones from my brother's kitchen." Selina attempted her own small joke. To her delight, he grinned.

"I am part Scotsman, my lady. I would never turn down such largesse."

"A Scotsman? I detect no sign of an accent."

David shrugged. "My mother's family comes from the lowlands, but she died when I was young. My English father ensured no trace of an accent remained."

"I'm sorry, David. I did not mean to distress you."

"Oh, Selina, it was many years ago. I have a few memories of my mother, but thoughts of her don't distress me." He looked up the stairs. "But perhaps it would be best if I take you upstairs. I'll let you find your own room from there. It would not be proper else."

He paused, then almost whispered. "Am I forgiven for my awkward phrasings?"

Selina nodded. "Of course. Now let us to our beds and hope for a more unruffled tomorrow."

CHAPTER FOUR

When David woke and looked out the window in his bedroom, he discovered that white blanketed the grounds of Wakefield Hall. The snow was still falling heavily from a gray sky, and the green boughs of the firs bowed down with the weight on their limbs.

He was used to snowy weather, but the expanses of white took his breath away. His house in Carlisle had only a small yard where any snow soon turned to dirty grime from the soot and dirt, and in Edinburgh, he owned a townhouse. Looking out at the park made him long for the fields around the village where he grew up, where he could run with the other children, building forts and throwing snowballs at each other.

He could certainly afford a country estate as his investments were hugely profitable. For just a minute he imagined children playing on a lawn of his own, Lion running around them while a laughing woman with brown curls watched.

The holidays were making him maudlin. David shook his head and turned away from the window to go down to the breakfast room.

He enjoyed his life as it was — didn't he? He was a busy and respected man with good friends. If, occasionally, he wished for a woman of his own at his table and in his bed, well, he had time yet. He had only just entered his third decade. Soon he would look for a possible wife among his associates, someone who understood the world he lived in and could entertain for him, give him children who would grow up to inherit the business he had built.

He made his way to the breakfast room to find the other men already sitting and enjoying their meal.

"There he is," Jamie said as he looked up. "We were wondering when you were planning to come down to eat."

David took a plate and surveyed the offerings. The Earl, or his cook, set out an exceptional array of food for his guests.

"It's early yet. I did not expect you gentlemen to have arisen this soon." He found a place at the table and unfolded his napkin. "I assume the ladies are taking trays in their rooms?"

Aubrey grunted. "As all three of our wives are currently anticipating a blessed event, I, for one, would be happy if Lucy could stomach the sight of a tray, much less eat from one."

Jamie nodded his head, and Richard pushed his plate away as if in sympathy with his wife.

"My congratulations," David said. "My feeble understanding of such matters is that this uneasy time will pass —soon, I hope, for your sakes."

He took a bite, then asked in a casual manner that fooled no one, "And what of Lady Selina? I hope both she and her mother have recovered after their travel."

"My understanding is they also took trays, but are both feeling more the thing this morning," Richard answered.

David nodded and applied himself to his plate. He hadn't expected Selina would be at the breakfast table as ladies of the Ton often broke their fasts with trays in their rooms, but at least it sounded as if she was feeling more robust today.

"I was hoping to go for a ride this morning, but I'm afraid the weather will prevent that activity," Richard noted.

"Perhaps the snow will slow or even stop," Jamie mused.

"It delights Lucy. She enjoys a fresh coat of snow for Christmas, no matter how bad it might obstruct the roads. I plan to take Annabelle out later. Perhaps it will tire her out. Her glee at spending time here with her cousin can be too exuberant at times." Aubrey quirked a wry grin as he set down his teacup.

"I might take Ned out for a short while to join her if his mother and nurse approve. I am at their disposal in all matters regarding my son." Richard sat back in his chair and rested his hands on his stomach, the very picture of a gentleman at his leisure. David could admire that, even as he realized that he sat erect in his chair as his father taught him he should.

Perhaps that was the clear difference between those of noble rank who attended Eton, and one raised in genteel poverty with a good education. Maybe it was all a matter of posture, he thought to himself with a laugh.

"What about you, David? I hear you have an addition to your family?" Richard said with a smile. "I'm sure Annabelle would love to meet your new dog."

"New dog?" Jamie asked. "How did that happen? There was no dog in my coach when we arrived."

David explained how the dog had approached Selina in the garden the day before, and how she had removed the thorn in its paw. He related humorously how he had ended up with the animal, but skipped the scene in the stables.

The men all laughed at his befuddlement at somehow gaining a large pet, quite amused at his predicament.

"Well, he's made good friends with Cook who allowed him to remain in the kitchen last night," Richard said. "However, I assured her that Lion belonged to you and would not be staying past the new year's beginning."

David chuckled. "Yes, I agreed to take charge of Lion, but if Cook insists on keeping him..." More laughter as Richard sputtered and waved his hands in protest.

The men continued to talk, lingering over their coffee and tea. David could see the other three were comfortable with each other, and it pleased him they included him as an equal. He would never forget that he wasn't on the same social level as these noblemen, but he appreciated their kindness. They asked him questions, not just about business, but about himself, his likes, his life. It was clear they were genuinely interested.

He had always been a loner, but David found he liked having friends. And he thought he could consider these men friends.

SELINA USUALLY AROSE early in the day, but today she slept in and then enjoyed her breakfast in the comfort of her room. It surprised her when the maid pulled back the drapes, showing the heavy snow falling. Her room looked out toward the rear of the estate, where the gardens were sited. Snow now covered the path she had walked yesterday.

She traced a finger on the cold glass. She would like to have gone out for another walk today, but her bad leg made walking through drifts of heavy snow impossible.

Any fantasies of running into David outside once again dissipated into the crystal swirls in the gray air. A feeling of restlessness made her feel trapped. Selina closed her eyes and took a deep breath, her usual solution for what was often a familiar feeling.

Quickly dressing, she crossed the hall to check on her mother. A quick knock and she opened the door to find Bevins bustling around the room while Mama ate from her tray, her back against a mountain of pillows. Bevins must have requisitioned pillows from every empty room in the place.

"Good morning, Mama. How are you feeling this morning?"

Her mother smiled; apparently, the rest had done her some good.

"Selina, love, I'm feeling much better. I daresay this bed may be one of the most comfortable I've ever slept in."

Selina raised an eyebrow, amazed at her mother's conciliatory tone. She had been prepared for more complaints, not praise. Perhaps Mama had changed her mind about the company.

"I'm glad, Mama." She dragged a chair next to the bed and sat. "Have you seen the snow?"

Her mother airily waved a hand. "No, but Bevins mentioned it. I suppose we are here for a fortnight so what does it matter as long as it's gone when we wish to return south."

"I love seeing snow for the holidays." Selina hid a grin when Bevins sniffed and slammed a drawer. Bevins was from Dorset, a true southerner who thought London qualified as the 'North' and shuddered when she found out they were traveling to Yorkshire.

"It *is* festive." Her mother shrugged. "No matter, I am resigned to our stay. I had hoped there would be a few eligible gentlemen here for you to meet, and perhaps some neighbors may visit later in the week. We can look forward to that, at least."

David is eligible, Selina thought, then blinked. Her mother would never see him as a gentleman. She was old-fashioned about that sort of thing.

Besides, why did it matter? It wasn't as if he were interested in Selina. They had just met, and he was polite. A kind man. A handsome man.

She couldn't help thinking about David while Bevins helped her mother to dress. He must be an extraordinary man to have gained a Duke's attention. Jamie seemed to think a lot of him. Eleanor, also, seemed to like him. Though he was a very likable man.

"You're silent this morning, Selina. Did you sleep well?" Her mother was ready to go downstairs.

"Yes, fine. Just woolgathering, Mama."

Selina followed her mother out of the room, taking her arm to help her down the hallway. Her mother allowed it, thinking Selina needed the support, but, in truth, it was Mama who was often unsteady. She suffered from an imbalance in the ears that caused her to misstep sometimes. At least Selina would use her cane; Mama refused to believe she had any issues despite several minor falls.

Descending the stairs to the main hall, Selina saw David waiting at the bottom. He had a slight smile on his face, and he fixed his eyes on her, but she didn't feel as if he was merely worried about her leg giving out. No, he just looked happy to see her.

She felt her mother stiffen as they neared the bottom of the staircase and she caught sight of the man waiting for them.

"Good morning, Lady Ludlow, Selina. I hope you've both recovered from your journey."

Selina smiled and opened her mouth to reply when her mother hissed, "That's Lady Selina, Mr. Gray."

David's face reddened at the rebuke, and Selina's heart sank.

"No, Mama, that's not so." Her voice faltered, but then she firmed her spine and continued, "Last evening we agreed to address each other by our given names rather than titles. Our party is informal, and all are good friends."

"Selina, that is not proper. You don't even know this man." Her mother darted a contemptuous look at David. He had stepped back, his face solemn. The hurt in his eyes made Selina's heart ache.

"Not well, true, but we have begun an acquaintance." She took a deep breath. "David is a good man and a true friend to the Duke of Carlisle." She grimaced, hoping that David understood the reference to Jamie's title was to appease her mother.

The Dowager Countess tightened her lips and stepped down to the floor. She glanced at David but didn't speak further, just bypassed him as she sailed down the corridor toward the sitting room. Selina glanced nervously, but her mother never looked back.

"I'm so sorry."

"It's all right. Your mother is entitled to her opinion." The tightness around David's eyes made Selina's stomach roil.

"She is very set in her ways, somewhat old-fashioned." She pressed her free hand to her stomach as if that might settle it.

David leaned forward and whispered, "I don't think she likes me."

"Oh." Selina was mortified until she realized David was joking. The tension had left his face, and one corner of his mouth was tipped up in a grin.

"Perhaps." Selina would not lie. David was too intelligent to dupe with a weak falsehood.

"Please don't worry. I can understand your mother's feelings in this. I admit I'm somewhat uncomfortable about addressing you this way myself, but I'll cede to the request of my hosts."

Just then there was a heavy pounding on the front door. Selina and David turned as Williams darted out of a side room to answer the knocking. A man fell through the door as soon as it opened, his greatcoat and hat covered in the snow that was still falling outside.

"Is your master at home? I need some help," he said, looking around the hall. He looked at Selina and David for a long moment but then turned back to Williams impatiently. "Well?"

Williams waited to take his wet outerwear but bowed and answered, "Of course, my lord. Let me fetch him." He hurried off, giving quick instruction to a footmen who came forward to aid the man in his stead.

Once he had removed his coat, hat, and scarf, the man came forward to where Selina and David stood.

"Lady Selina, I did not expect to see you here." He was a thin man with a long aristocratic nose, impeccably dressed though his face was still ruddy from the cold.

"My lord," Selina curtsied. "May I introduce Mr. Gray of Carlisle, also a guest of the Earl of Wakefield?"

The man shot him a quick glance and nodded, dismissing David rudely. Selina felt her neck grow hot as anger and embarrassment warred in her breast. David gave a short bow but offered nothing of what he was thinking.

"Mr. Gray, this is the Earl of Warham." She knew her tone was too curt, but Lucien Fox had always given her a bad feeling. He ignored her when their paths crossed at balls or musical performances, but she had heard stories of his gambling and profligacy. His rapier wit was well-known in the Ton but was usually wielded against the defenseless. He was cruel, not at all the kind of person that Richard would associate with.

Still, he had his followers. His appearance and manners fooled many people, at least until he had taken their fortune at the gambling tables or ruined their reputation by whispered gossip.

Richard appeared, followed by Williams. His manners were too good to betray his feelings toward his unexpected guest, but Selina noticed he wasn't enthused in his greetings.

"Warham, this is a surprise. I understand you need my help."

"Yes, I do. My coach has broken down a short way down the road, a wheel broken when my inept coachman drove into a ditch. I'll need lodgings until the snow stops and I can send him to get a new wheel or make repairs." He tugged at a sleeve, his features displaying boredom.

Selina could see he had no concern for any inconvenience he might be imposing. Apparently, he had forced his coachman out in the bad weather and now blamed him for the mishap with the coach.

"Of course," Richard answered. "I'll send some men out to fetch your coachman and horses also. I'm sure they'll want a warm, dry place out of the weather also. Meanwhile, can I offer you hospitality, some food? I expect you haven't broken your fast yet this morning."

Warham was staring at Selina, an odd look in his eyes. She felt uncomfortable and glanced away.

He turned back to Richard at his words and answered, "I would be grateful for something warm to eat, and I would like to meet the rest of your party as it appears I may be your guest for the next few days."

As they followed Williams down the hall, Selina heard Warham say to Richard, "Perhaps this accident has been most opportune."

A shiver ran down her spine. Somehow she knew this did not bode well for her.

CHAPTER FIVE

David sipped from his glass, observing the room over the edge from his place near the fireplace. The house party had gathered after dinner into small groups, engaged in conversation while the piano was set up and chairs arranged. Anne had decided that music would be an excellent evening entertainment.

Usually, David enjoyed a musical evening, but his sense of discomfort had been increasing from the time of the Earl of Warham's arrival, and it dampened his pleasure in the company.

With the snow still falling, it confined everyone indoors. The ladies had been busy with visits to the nursery, needlework, and conversation. When the gentlemen joined them later in the afternoon, he had found Selina reading a book, but she placed it on a nearby table when she saw him standing close by. She smiled and greeted him, but her mother called to her, asking her to sit next to her on a sofa across the room. She gave a small frown but did as her mother asked.

The Dowager Countess had made it obvious she didn't like him. He could understand her views logically, but his lonely heart rebelled. David enjoyed his conversations with Selina, found her gentleness attractive, and felt protective of her. He would like to know her better, but her mother's attitude discouraged any friendship and made him sad.

To his dismay, it appeared she found the Earl of Warham a more attractive prospect for her daughter, despite Selina's clear reluctance for his attention. Even worse, the Earl seemed willing to agree to the Dowager's wishes. He came across the room to sit on Selina's other side, much too close, in David's opinion, for good manners.

Selina looked tense and unhappy. She didn't take part in the conversation, letting it flow over her between her mother and the Earl. She kept her eyes fixed on the carpet, twisting the head of her cane in her hands.

David didn't know much about the Earl of Warham. He wasn't part of the Ton and didn't follow the gossip sheets. But there was something about the man's looks he didn't like, an arrogant set to his aristocratic features, and something more. Cruelty? Dissipation? David wasn't sure, but he trusted his feelings. Warham was not a good man.

"You're brooding." Jamie had come up behind him.

"No, not at all," David responded.

Jamie lifted one ducal eyebrow, his doubt on full display.

"Well, perhaps a little," David conceded. There was no point in hiding his distrust of the man monopolizing Selina's attention. "What do you know about the Earl of Warham?"

"Hmmm," Jamie grunted, then turned, so his back was to those seated on the sofa. "His title is old and his family respected."

David nodded, a sinking feeling in his stomach.

"But the present Earl is of a different mode than the rest of his relatives. All know him as a spendthrift, a gambler whose affairs are in disrepair. He's been selling off anything not entailed but is still deeply in debt. The last rumors I'd heard have him attempting to repair his fortune by marriage to an heiress. There was a girl he was wooing. Her father has a fortune in wool though her breeding is not equal to his own."

David didn't take the last comment amiss as the Duke had married a woman that society would consider far beneath himself. But the rest of Jamie's disclosures disquieted him. He understood Selina was an heiress, prey for a man like Warham.

He trusted her good sense, but her mother seemed the type more concerned with consequence and could put considerable pressure on her daughter. The situation made him uneasy.

"Gentleman, ladies, I believe we are finally ready." Anne stood by the piano, cool and elegant in a blue evening gown. "Lucy has agreed to start off the festivities."

Lucy seated herself, her husband at her side to act as a page turner, and played a lively short piece by Haydn. She performed credibly, David thought, though it was clear she was not an accomplished performer. Aubrey rewarded her with a quick kiss on her hand, obviously proud of his wife.

Her brother Richard took a seat next, playing a lovely version of Beethoven's Piano Concerto 1 with style and grace to much applause by the company. It was a long piece, and David kept stealing glances at Selina. She still looked anxious, sitting with her shoulders stiff. She didn't take her eyes off Richard as he played.

Warham leaned back slightly, his fingers tapping on the arm of the sofa though not in time with the music. It was more from boredom, David thought. His face was impassive, with an occasional look at Selina sitting next to him.

"Selina, can we prevail on you to sing if someone accompanies you? You have such a lovely voice," Anne asked.

Selina stood and went to the piano, shuffling through the sheet music on a table next to it while Anne looked around the room for a volunteer.

"I'd be willing to play for the lady." It amazed David to hear his voice ring out.

Anne smiled. "Thank you. That would be lovely."

Sweating, David walked to the piano and addressed Selina. "It appears I am to accompany you. What have you chosen?"

She blushed and held out a paper. David saw it was the Coventry Carol.

"I thought perhaps some Christmas music would be appropriate."

He smiled. "I know it well." He seated himself on the bench and waited for her to signal she was ready.

In truth, David found the time to play the piano almost every day. His father had ensured he had lessons, and David loved to practice. He played well, though rarely in company.

Selina lifted her chin, and he pressed down on the keys as she sang. She had a lovely alto voice that fit the carol perfectly. She turned her head to look at him when he joined in on the chorus, singing the harmony in his deep baritone, and didn't move her eyes away from him until the song ended, the last notes quietly fading.

"Thank you," she whispered as the room applauded.

"It is my great pleasure," he said, and he dared to kiss her gloved fingertips. Her rosy blush was his reward.

The Earl of Warham interrupted them. He took Selina's arm, subtly inserting himself between them.

"My dear, what a lovely voice you have. It would be heaven to hear it every day."

Selina's eyes widened. "Thank you, my lord." David thought she tried to pull away, but Warham wouldn't let go of her arm. Instead, he turned to David.

"Perhaps Mr. Gray would play more. We all enjoyed his performance and would like to hear more."

David replied, "I'd be glad to play more carols, and we can all sing."

"That's a wonderful idea," Anne said from her place on the sofa. "Everyone, let us gather around the piano. Some carols would be festive. Let us be merry."

David led the company in several carols. They sang joyfully except Selina who looked miserable and Warham who looked triumphant. Jamie and Lucy sang the loudest; the Duke had an excellent tenor and Lucy a sweet soprano, but there were no wrong notes from anyone.

David could think of no way to remove Selina from Warham's clutches, but she resolved the matter herself. After a few songs, she murmured about a headache and slipped from the room. Neither her mother or Warham looked pleased, but there was little either could do about it.

A few songs later, David yielded his place at the piano to Richard. He sang by rote, his brain engaged elsewhere. Selina may not be for him, but he would not let Warham have her either, since it only appeared he was just interested in her money. She deserved better than a man like the Earl.

SELINA SLIPPED INTO the hallway and hurried toward the library. Anne had just whispered in her ear that Warham was on his way into the house. The snow had finally stopped overnight, and he and Richard had gone to find out what was needed to fix his coach.

She thought he wouldn't look in the library for her, and her mother had gone upstairs for a rest. The two of them were determined to make her insane, she thought, never leaving her alone over the last day. Her mother kept espousing the virtues of the Earl, though Selina knew better, and the Earl was ever solicitous, standing much too close and making her uncomfortable.

It did no good to explain to her mother that the man was desperate for money. She had replied it didn't matter, Selina needed a husband. Nor did Warham seem to take any hints she wasn't interested in him.

The other women had been working on decorating the house for Christmas. Some of the servants had gone out earlier and brought back greens and mistletoe. Selina was enjoying spending time with Anne and her friends, and she loved hanging the fragrant pine boughs and holly branches with their scarlet berries.

But she knew Warham would make his way to her once he returned, and she determined to foil him. If David had been in the room, she might have stayed, but he had disappeared after lunch. They had sat together and had a pleasant conversation despite constant interruptions from her mother. Why Mama couldn't lose her blinders and see that David was the better man was beyond Selina's comprehension, but her mother had always been more of a snob. Her brother William, the current Earl of Ludlow, had married the daughter of a baronet. Margaret came from respectable stock, but while Mama liked her now, she had been very against the marriage at first.

Closing the library door, Selina breathed a sigh of relief. There was a fire burning in the hearth, and she could find a book to curl up with in the chair in front. She thought no one would see her there unless they came right over to it.

She chose the first book she found, a slim volume of Byron poems she had read before and liked, then limped over to the fireplace. It was better for her to sit for a while; she had stood for quite a while as they twisted the pine branches together.

She dropped the book with a cry when she realized someone already sat in the chair. David rose and gave a small bow, then picked up the volume from the floor.

"Selina, my pardon. I didn't mean to startle you."

"It's not your fault. I expected no one else to be in here."

He looked at her shrewdly and said, "Hiding, my dear?" He grinned, and Selina felt her stomach unknot. It was a wonder how David knew her so well after only a few days.

He moved aside and motioned for her to take the armchair where he had been sitting, then pulled another one over to sit near her by the fire. She sat, resting her cane against the chair arm and with her book in her lap. It wasn't proper for the two of them to be in here together with the door closed, but she didn't care.

David had a thick tome, marked by one finger to hold his place, but he didn't reopen the book, just sat in comfortable silence.

"What are you reading, if I may ask?" Selina inquired.

"A treatise on land management," David answered. "I find myself thinking about acquiring a small estate, not as big as Wakefield Hall. The call of country living has been strong, and my stay here only amplified that desire, despite the snow."

"You own two homes already, I believe." His comments intrigued Selina.

"Yes, but with minimal land. Lion would not cope well at either place, I think."

Selina laughed. "Are you telling me you plan to buy an estate for Lion?"

He turned red but shrugged. "For both Lion and myself. I need to take more time to relax, and it's hard to get away from business in the city." He leaned forward slightly. "Do you enjoy the country, Selina?"

She caught her breath. She felt the question had a deeper meaning. Rubbing at the cover of her book, Selina took a moment to gather her thoughts.

"Yes, I've always preferred the country. While the city has many entertainments, I feel freer at Ludlow Abbey, more myself. I don't know how to explain it." She frowned. "Perhaps it's because I'm more of a solitary creature. William, my brother, was older, not inclined to humor his little sister, so I was often on my own. I'm limited in what activities I can pursue, so I spend a lot of time walking. The country views are preferable for walking, and I need no one else to accompany me as I do in town."

"Yes, I am finding the view much better here than in Edinburgh or Carlisle." David was gazing steadily at her, and Selina grew warm — not just from the fire.

She didn't reply, more befuddled than anything, but David misinterpreted her silence.

"I apologize, I am too forward." He rose, but she grasped his hand, and he paused.

"No, not at all." She swallowed, her throat dry, and then found her courage. "I admit, though we have not known each other long, I find you..." she searched for an appropriate word, "very comfortable to be with also."

"Only comfortable?" he asked in a low tone.

"And uncomfortable." He sat back, his brow furrowed, and she longed to reach out and smooth it. "I only mean you bring up feelings I never felt before. I don't know how to process them."

"But they are uncomfortable? Because I would never want you to be uneasy because of me."

Selina laughed. "Oh, no. Warham makes me uneasy. I am only uncomfortable with you because," she took a deep breath, "I wish for more."

His dear face lit up with joy. "Is it possible? I am not of your rank. Your mother does not approve of me."

"My mother is overzealous but does not speak for me. She has always been too ambitious for me, partly because of her own upbringing, but also because she feels guilt for my lameness. It was not her fault, just a childhood illness, but Mama takes the blame for it on herself. My brother William is much like you, and I think you will find him much more accepting than my mother."

"Then will you allow me to court you, Selina? It is too soon for more, but I would like to know the possibility of more exists."

"Yes, I would like you to court me." Selina felt her heart might burst from happiness. Something about David made her bold; she couldn't imagine this conversation with another man. "I would ask if we could keep it between us until after the holidays. And it would please William if you wrote and asked him for permission."

"I will," David promised. He took her hand and stroked it gently. He looked absolutely blissful."

"I will ask him to invite you to Ludlow Abbey if you can spare the time."

"Yes, I will make arrangements." He smiled, his eyes crinkled with happiness. "I couldn't court you as well from Carlisle. And I wish to spend more time with you, to allow you to know me, to discover the kind of man I am."

"I believe I know very well what a good man you are."

David leaned forward and met her lips with his own. The kiss was brief but warm, their mouths aligning perfectly. Selina wished it could be longer, but David was a gentleman.

And he was hers.

CHAPTER SIX

The next few days flew by. David and Selina could spend private time together despite the best efforts of her mother and the Earl of Warham. True, David wasn't happy to see Warham monopolize much of her time, but Selina and he met in the library every afternoon where they could converse and share gentle kisses.

Selina found David to be all she wanted and more. He was intelligent, well versed in literature and music. He listened to her opinions respectfully, unlike many men in the Ton, and would be a good partner for her. In time, they might find their way to love, a prospect that made Selina's heart race.

She had always wanted love in her marriage. While her prospects had been few, it was partly because she was not willing to concede on romance. David was affectionate, and sometimes Selina thought she saw more in his eyes when he looked at her. There was no doubt he wasn't interested in her rank or her money. He was wealthy enough on his own. He respected those who he felt deserved his admiration, but David did not esteem those who were deliberately unkind or unfeeling.

Indeed, her own feelings toward David were growing. Selina could only admire his kindnesses, his honesty, and his quiet affection. She also thought him handsome which worried her. While she didn't doubt his feelings, she considered herself plain. He didn't seem bothered by her infirmity, but she couldn't help but wish she was a beauty like Lucy or even classically pretty like Anne. She felt petty, but at least he seemed to find her attractive.

Selina put on her pelisse and warm clothes. The last few days had warmed, the sun was bright, and much of the snow had melted away though one still couldn't see the ground. Anne had decided she wanted more greens for decorations, and the house party was spending time outdoors, doing her bidding. Mama had declined, opting to pass the time inside, but the rest of the adults and Annabelle were looking forward to breathing fresh air and getting out in the sun.

She joined the others in the foyer. David was talking to Aubrey and Lucy, but he glanced her way with the smile he saved only for her. She moved toward him, but Warham intercepted her before she could reach him.

"My lady," he said as he took her arm. "Perhaps you'll join me on this outing."

She hesitated, looking beyond him, but he turned her away.

"Your mother asked me to look out for you, and I am always happy to oblige."

"Thank you, my lord," she answered, knowing she had no choice. His carriage had been fixed two days ago, and why he continued to discommode his host no one knew. Supposedly, he had been on his way to a friend's home. She and she suspected the rest of the house party, wished he would resume his journey.

They moved outside, Annabelle skipping ahead of the rest. Two of the footmen hauled a large sled with tools.

Selina hated walking with Warham. He never seemed to realize she couldn't walk as fast as the others, pulling her along like a dray team with a heavy wagon. She did the best she could and finally stopped, digging her cane into the snow.

"My lord, please. I must walk a bit slower." Her anger overcame her embarrassment as two spots of red heated her cheeks.

"My apologies, Lady Selina." The rogue didn't sound sorry at all. "I didn't mean to hurry you. I thought you'd like to keep up with the others."

The others were almost out of sight, nearly to the woods. David was trailing them, Lion at his side. Selina saw him look back, and her heart warmed knowing he was watching out for her. Lion ran again toward her but heeled as David called out.

"What an ugly beast Mr. Gray has," Warham remarked. "I wonder he owns such a beast."

"Somehow Lion was injured, and Mr. Gray kindly took him in at my request," Selina replied stiffly. "I find his gesture generous toward a dumb animal and his nature most humane."

Warham raised an eyebrow. "I suppose, but he could have given the dog off to a farm or somewhere more appropriate."

Selina tightened her lips together, afraid she might say something rude. What an unfeeling man the Earl of Warham was! She couldn't wait for him to be on his way.

By now they had reached the others who were spreading out throughout the woods at Anne's direction.

"My lord, perhaps you would gather mistletoe for the hall," Anne said to Warham. The mistletoe was in a grove of oaks some way away from where they stood. She and Anne had planned for Selina to plead the length of the walk to keep from having to accompany him.

"Lady Selina and I live to serve you," with only a hint of sarcasm in his voice, Warham answered.

Selina demurred, but Warham kept a firm grasp on her arm and pulled her along. "Lady Selina, since you know the way, I insist you accompany me."

Anne bit her lip unhappy at the Earl's persistence, and she looked to David for salvation. She held a canvas bag meant to keep the mistletoe, and David took it from her.

"I'd be glad to help gather mistletoe. Another set of hands is always helpful, and I'm sure Lady Anne is looking for a great quantity to decorate the hall."

Warham snatched the bag away. "That is unnecessary, sir. Lady Selina and I have it all to hand." His face was implacable, and Selina, who had calmed when David stepped in, felt her heart sink.

Selina was raised as a lady. Her mother told her not to argue with a gentleman, but to accede to his wishes if possible. Her infirmity made her even more timid about asserting herself, but she wished, just for once, that she could stamp her foot and refuse. It was remarkable she felt so comfortable with David that she never needed to resort to meekness.

Most of the rest of the party had disappeared into the woods, and she could hear their calls as they fell to their tasks. They would not be too far away, and she knew David would stay close, even if Warham had refused his aid.

Agreeing to the inevitable, Selina said, "Shall we go then, my lord?"

The snow barely covered the ground under the trees, and Warham, pleased he had won the confrontation, graciously slowed for her. As the terrain was uneven and covered with roots, Selina was happy for her cane and even the Earl's arm. The sooner she could get this excursion over with, the sooner she could meet David in the library.

It was a beautiful day. The sun warmed her shoulders, even under the trees. The snow left a freshness to the landscape that cheered her and buoyed her spirits despite her companion.

"The oak grove is just ahead," she said, pointing toward it with her cane. "I can see clumps of mistletoe adhering to some of the lower branches."

The Earl was a tall man, and despite his clear disdain for his task, he could reach and pull down healthy masses of the greens. Selina's job was to stuff them into the sack until it was bulging.

"There, I believe we have enough," she said wiping her gloved hands together. "If you would be so good as to carry the sack, we can rejoin the others."

"Just a moment, if you would, Lady Selina. I have something I wish to say to you."

Selina turned, startled and dismayed. She had no desire to linger further with the Earl and hoped to tamp down any personal conversation, but he had a look of determination on his face that boded ill. Egged on by her mother, she feared he would offer matrimony. She took a deep breath and attempted to gain a resolve of her own.

Thoughts of David steadied her. She would politely tell the Earl no, that she already had an understanding with a different gentleman who she loved. Selina's eyes widened as she realized — she loved David!

She wanted to tell him, and she glanced toward where their footsteps in the snow displayed the path she should follow to find him. She looked up to see the Earl was studying her, his face thoughtful.

"Lady Selina, you are an intelligent woman. You know what I will say to you." He reached out and put a finger under her chin, lifting her face. "You think to refuse me, stupidly intent on a man below your rank."

He laughed at her bewilderment. "You think I am not aware of your secret meetings with Mr. Grey each afternoon? It matters not to me for you will be my wife regardless. I care not if you come to my bed unblemished or not, once the marriage contracts are signed."

Horrified, Selina tried to draw back, but he grasped her by the shoulders.

"I will not be your wife. I will marry Mr. Gray!"

"Your mother assures me that will never happen," he sneered. "She looks with favor on my suit."

"My brother is head of the family, and he will decide. He will never choose a husband for me who is only interested in my money."

"What if he has no choice?"

Selina belatedly realized he intended to compromise her. She wasn't clear on how he meant to accomplish it amidst the snow and wet ground, but all he needed to do was rip her clothing and give the appearance of a ravishment, and it would seal her fate. She tried to step back, but he held her tight.

As he loomed over her, she brought her cane up and dealt him a blow on the head. He dropped his hands, stupefied, then reached up to where drops of blood trickled down his forehead. He touched the spot, then brought his glove down to see the blood staining the leather.

"You bit-" he cut off as Lion burst into the clearing and jumped on him, knocking him to the ground. The dog growled, showing his teeth. Warham was using blasphemies Selina had never heard before, even on the streets of London, but he could not move out from under the dog. Lion didn't bite, but the threat was there.

"Selina! Are you all right?" Suddenly David was there, his arms around her waist, and Selina's world settled. She clung to him, her head resting on his chest, listening to the rapid beats of his heart. He had raced to find her.

"Get your bloody dog off me, Gray!"

David kept his hold on Selina, but he whistled for Lion. The dog came to his side, keeping an eye on Warham, ready to resume his place on the Earl's chest if needed.

The man scrambled up. He was a mess. Blood and mud splattered his clothing and face, his hair disarranged in wild swirls, and his face was red with rage.

"How dare you?" he sputtered. "Unhand Lady Selina this moment. She is my affianced!"

Selina tensed and shook her head frantically, but David answered for her.

"I'm afraid that's impossible, my lord. The lady has already agreed to marry me. Your behavior toward my betrothed is more than unseemly. I will meet you tomorrow morning to settle this matter."

Selina gasped. David could not fight a duel over her. What if he was injured or worse, killed?

"I will not fight you, Gray," the Earl said contemptuously. "You are not a gentleman, and I will not meet with you." He brushed dirt off his coat, appearing to calculate his choices. "Very well, if you want her, take her. The money would be helpful to my present circumstances but doesn't compensate for her obvious disadvantages. I have other options."

David stepped forward and very neatly clipped the Earl across the jaw, sending him to the ground once again.

"Since I am not a gentleman in your eyes, I suppose my behavior is only expected," David said. "I love Selina, and I will not tolerate any gossip or disparagement about her. She is perfect, and I am humbled to think she would be my wife. Say one more word about her, and I will meet with you, gentleman or not. And I am a dead shot, sir."

"Come, love," he said as he took her arm and picked up the sack of mistletoe from the ground. "The others are awaiting our return."

They walked away, not seeing Lion perform one final act of vengeance and lift his leg on the Earl's boots.

CHAPTER SEVEN

The Earl departed the party that afternoon, not saying a word to anyone including his hosts. The Dowager Countess of Ludlow mourned his leave-taking, and she suspected the blame lay upon her daughter.

Selina didn't care.

David had said he loved her. She hadn't a chance to speak to let him know she reciprocated his feelings, but she had hidden a sprig of mistletoe away for their next meeting in the library.

First, she had to explain to Anne what had occurred in the woods. Warham's behavior outraged her, and she was upset she hadn't done something more to forestall him.

"I swear, Selina if I thought he would behave like that, I would have had Richard throw him out days ago. I'm so sorry you had to go through that." Anne grasped her hands, overwrought that her friend had gone through such unpleasantness.

"Anne, do not distress yourself. David and Lion saved me." Selina squeezed Anne's hands. "I would never have married him anyway, no matter the disgrace. I'd rather have been ruined."

Anne sighed and shook her head. "It never would have come to that. David would have married you regardless if you'd have him."

Selina blushed but didn't answer. Instead, she gave Anne a reassuring hug.

"Thank you again for everything. The hall looks wonderful, so imbued with holiday spirit."

Diverted, Anne rattled on about her plans for Christmas. Rather than holding a ball, she and Richard had decided to open the hall for their tenants. They would provide food and drink—and some largesse, Selina thought — for their people in honor of the holiday. They would also invite the neighbors, but Richard was more concerned about his people.

Selina tried to listen, but her attention was on the china clock on the mantle of Anne's sitting room. Anne must have noticed for she fell quiet.

"I'm sorry, Anne. I've been woolgathering. What were you saying?"

"I said I think you need a rest before dinner. After all that happened today, of course, you are distracted and tired. Go on upstairs, and I'll make sure you are called in time to dress for dinner." Anne smiled and patted her hand.

Selina rose, but once she reached the hallway, she gave a quick look around and headed for the library, trying not to let her cane tap on the marble floor and give her whereabouts away.

David rose almost immediately when she entered and came to greet her, taking her hands and drawing her to their usual chairs by the fireplace.

"I thought you might be resting. I would not blame you if you wanted to take the opportunity —"

Selina leaned forward and put her fingers to his lips. "Of course, I would come to meet you today. I'm not so fragile that a little misadventure would overset me so." She explained, "I delayed to speak with Anne. She feels guilty though this incident was no fault of hers."

"The fault is mine. I should never have allowed Warham to escort you today." His face was grim, and Selina reached up to lay a hand on his cheek. He took her hand and kissed the palm, carefully closing her fingers over the soft caress.

"You had no way to know..."

"No, I knew he would propose soon. I received information that showed his finances were in dire straits through Jamie's contacts. I didn't know how desperate he was." David swallowed hard, his face pale in the ruddy light of the fire. "If the circumstances had been different, he could have done you great harm, Selina."

"But he didn't. I am sturdier than you think," she said. "I managed to strike a blow with my cane before Lion — and you — came to my rescue."

He was still holding her hand, but Selina needed to be closer. She also hoped to divert him, so she climbed into his lap and nestled herself comfortably, leaning her head against his chest.

"Selina, what if someone comes in?" David asked though she thought him amused at her boldness.

"The Earl of Warham informed " that everyone in the house already knows we meet in the library each afternoon." She giggled. "Except my mother."

"What?" he sputtered. "I never meant for anyone to think badly of you."

"Hush, David," Selina said. "Everyone here gives a courting couple a degree of license." She looked down at where their hands clasped together in her lap. "We are a courting couple, are we not?"

He kissed her forehead. "Did you not hear what I said to Warham? I told him we were to marry."

"Yes, you did." She looked up at him from under her eyelashes. "But I don't remember you asking me?"

David looked dumbfounded, but there was a twinkle in his eye. "Did I not? Please stand up, so I can kneel at your feet and rectify this situation."

She giggled, feeling light as a snowflake in the wind. He smiled, glad to see her so relaxed and happy.

"I will not make you kneel. I'm far too comfortable where I am."

"Then Lady Selina Masters, will you do me the great honor of becoming my wife, to protect and love for the rest of our lives?"

"Love?" she whispered.

"Ahhh," he said and pulled her closer. "I really must have a physician check your hearing. Didn't you hear me tell Warham today? I love you, Selina. I know you like me and I will work every day to earn your love one day."

"I *do* love you now, and I have for a while though I only realized it today." Selina dropped her head to his chest, but David put a finger under her chin and lifted her head up until she gazed at him.

"You love me? Oh, Selina, love," and his lips met hers in a firm kiss that lingered and grew until they broke apart, both breathing hard.

He tipped his head against the chair. "So, is that a yes?"

"Yes," she answered.

SELINA HAD DRESSED in one of her favorite gowns, a deep gold satin gown that set off her abundant brown hair. Bevins helped her twine a matching ribbon through her curls. The result pleased Selina ; she felt fresh and pretty, and ready to face her mother.

She had convinced David it would be better for her to speak to the Dowager alone first. The final answer was up to her brother William, and Selina knew William would agree to her marriage to David. He only wanted his sister's happiness.

But her mother was a different story.

Bevins had confided her mother waited for her to go down to dinner. It was early yet, and Selina would have enough time to tell her mother about her betrothal — but not enough time before dinner for her mother to marshal an argument.

She knocked on the door and entered her mother's bedroom. Her mother dressed in black and sat in a comfortable chair near the fireplace in her room. She looked weary and discouraged. Selina felt the nerves in her stomach give way to a pang of guilt. She loved her mother no matter how irritating Mama could be.

"Selina, how pretty you look."

"Thank you, Mama. You look very nice also." She took a deep breath, ready to launch into the speech she'd practiced, but her mother spoke first.

"Selina, I want to apologize to you. I have not put your best interests first, and I was wrong."

"What do you mean, Mama?" She sat on the edge of her mother's bed and leaned forward.

"I spoke to Anne this afternoon. She made clear the nature of the Earl of Warham's interest in you." Tears trickled down her face, and Selina jumped up to kneel at her mother's feet and took her hands into her own.

"I was so proud," her mother said. "I thought he admired you and would be a good match. Until Anne spoke to me, I did not understand what a wastrel he is." Her mother smoothed back a curl that had come loose behind Selina's ear. "You're so lovely, how could he not fall in love with you?"

"Mama, don't feel bad about Warham. He's fooled many members of the Ton over the years. I might have believed in his interest if mine own was not already engaged with another."

Her mother tensed, then seemed to sag in her chair. "Yes, Mr. Gray. Anne scolded me roundly, saying I haven't given him a chance. Dear Anne. So wise at her young years." She sighed and said, "I'd hoped you'd find a husband with a title as she did, but what matters is that you love him, and he loves you."

"I love him, Mama, and he loves me also, even in the short time we've known each other." Selina laid her head on her mother's lap. "He wants to marry me, Mama," she whispered.

The Dowager Countess rested a hand on Selina's head. "And you want to marry him also. This news will overjoy your brother. He's told me to let you be, that all would come right. And so it has." She reached for a handkerchief from the table next to her and wiped at her face.

"The gong has sounded, Mama. Are you ready to go down for dinner?" Selina asked as she lifted herself up with some effort and the help of her cane.

"Yes, I'm ready. I'd like to sit near Mr. Gray and converse with him. All these young people, Anne and William, showing me the way. Perhaps I can learn something from Mr. Gray also."

Selina laughed as she took her mother's arm. "I expect you both will learn something. But I depend on you to keep my secrets, Mama. No stories about how I misbehaved as a child as you did to Rose when she was betrothed to William."

"I would never do that," her mother said with a wink. "At least, until the betrothal is formal."

CHAPTER EIGHT

There was only one more day before Selina and her mother would head for Ludlow Abbey. Jamie and his wife, along with David, were leaving at the same time with a quick stop in York for Jamie to pick up a special license for the betrothed couple. As a Duke, he had the authority that David didn't.

The Dowager Countess had agreed after many protestations that a quick wedding in the chapel at Ludlow Abbey would do. While her mother initially opted for a grander ceremony in London once the season started, both David and Selina agreed they'd rather have a quiet nuptials with a few friends and relatives.

The holiday party for the tenants had gone well. The house party guests all mingled, Annabelle enjoying the chance to play with the other children. Ned tried to keep up with them but was soon turned over to his nurse, exhausted by the party. Richard and Anne were much loved by their people for their many kindnesses all year long, but everyone enjoyed the games and bountiful food and drink provided with merry Christmas spirit.

Selina and David took part, never far from each other as they wandered through the hall. When the impromptu band played a slow song, David took her hand and dragged her onto the dance floor.

"I don't dance," she protested.

"Never?" he asked.

She shook her head. "My leg," she reminded him.

"But you're dancing now."

She smiled. "I am, aren't I?"

They were quiet for a moment.

"Promise me?" David asked. "Promise you'll dance with me every Christmas for the rest of our lives?"

He slowed until they were standing under a clump of mistletoe. Selina looked up and laughed.

"I promise," she whispered as David kissed her.

Author's Note

Jerusha Moors grew up in Connecticut but currently lives in Portland, Maine. Her sister introduced her to the books of Georgette Heyer, and she never outgrew her love of romance books, especially from the Regency period. She hopes you enjoy her stories and books about those times and will follow her on social media.

She appreciates you sharing this adventure with her. She will continue to write about Regency romance. I appreciate any and all reviews. Thank you for reading!

Books by Jerusha Moors

Always – Richard and Anne's story (free short story)

Abandon – Aubrey and Lucy's story

Advantage – Jamie and Eleanor's story

The Handkerchief – a Regency short story (free)

Don't miss out!

Visit the website below and you can sign up to receive emails whenever Jerusha Moors publishes a new book. There's no charge and no obligation.

https://books2read.com/r/B-A-LAIH-AXFW

BOOKS 2 READ

Connecting independent readers to independent writers.